Secret of the
BLUEBONNET

The Legendary Love Story
That Created a Flower

RICK W. WILLIAMS

*Be advised: there are mild references to adult situations
and some violence necessary for story continuity.*

*In loving memory of my late grandmother,
Nola Estelle Taylor. As a kid, Gram taught me
how to fish, shoot, drive, and call roadrunners,
among many other things. She was tough,
plainspoken, fair-minded and she loved her
family very, very much. The most important life
rule I ever learned, she taught me. Gram would
often tell me, "You were given two eyes, two ears,
and two nostrils but only one mouth. What does
that tell you?" And I have lived a successful life
by understanding and applying that rule. I sorely
miss her strength, wisdom, and love.*

INTRODUCTION

This is the legend of a love story that my grandmother would tell us children every spring. Why would a bunch of squirmy kids sit still to listen to a love story? Well, first off, you had to know what a great storyteller my grandmother was. Second and most importantly, we knew that after hearing her tell the story, she would initiate—or reinitiate—us into the tiny, ultra-cool group of people that knew the *secret of the blue-bonnet*. The secret that proved the story was true…at least as far as *we* were concerned.

Unfortunately, this story's origins seem lost to the dust of history. I spent many years researching oral and written references to what few bluebonnet origin stories there are. And up to now, I have neither found nor heard anything akin to her story. My grandmother told us that her grandmother and her grandmother's grandmothers had passed down this story for longer than any of them could remember.

So, every year, usually on a sunny spring weekend or during a holiday, Gram would get us kids all together at her South Austin home and herd us out into her backyard, under a huge oak tree. We would all lay in the sun-dappled grass with our heads in a small circle around a sprig of bluebonnets she had designated. It was always done this way, so she could show us the secret without having to pick a flower. In Gram Taylor's world (and consequently ours), bluebonnets were only for "look'n at, not for pick'n." And woe unto anyone that ever broke this rule, and she found out.

Once all the giggling, the squirming, and the whispering subsided under a stern side-eyed look, she would take her place in the circle and tell us the story that gave Texas the bluebonnet. After it was finished, she would reach out to the bluebonnets we encircled and show us how to gently coax out the secret that existed in every bright blue and white blossom. With the hard truth staring us in the face, we all knew beyond a shadow of a doubt that her story *had* to be true.

Obviously, her story wasn't anywhere as detailed as it appears on the following pages, but the setting, the characters, and the outcome are just as they were in her oral version. I took her oral story, fleshed it out, put a little hair on it and put it down on paper for posterity. I don't think Gram would mind, as long as no bluebonnets were harmed or picked in the writing of this story.

I truly hope you enjoy reading this small piece of my family's history that I have carried in my heart since I was but a wee little Texan. And when you've finished, you too will have joined the ultra-cool group of people who know the legendary love story and the secret of the bluebonnet.

This one's for you, Gram.

It all started in a time long, long ago when the earth was younger, the heavens were bluer, and the Great Sky Spirit watched closely over his children with the soft eyes of a loving father. Men in the known world had just begun to explore their small part of the earth and had yet to even dream of the Great Land that lay far to the West, beyond the blue, serpent-filled ocean that fell into the sunset.

After many cold seasons, the children of the Great Sky Spirit had grown tired of following the giant buffalo herds that roamed the prairies. Seeing their weariness, the Great Sky Spirit guided them to a place where the earth was dark and rich, the forests were plentiful with game, and a swift, cold river filled a wide lake that stretched toward where the sun awakens each day.

The river was lined with tall trees that had gnarled roots, and it provided fish, mussels, and clay. The nearby lake held sweet clear water, and the fish were varied and plentiful. Along the lake's shore, reeds and cattails grew for making baskets, and in the neighboring lands were stands of oak, hickory, and other hardwood trees. An endless forest stood beside the lake that was home to bear, panther, deer, and beaver. It also grew all the wild berries, nuts, and mushrooms they could pick.

In the far North lay the home of the Blue Wolf, who brought the cold season and who sometimes left his soft white trail over the land to mark where he had traveled.

Closer, the Great Prairie was home to black herds of buffalo. The herds could churn the grassy prairie into black earth for as far as the eye could see, fill the air with thunder, and make dust so thick that it looked like the Great Sky Spirit had set the land on fire.

Every day, the sun awoke in the east, where endless pine forests, great rivers, and dark, forbidding swamps spread endlessly. In the western lands, where the sun slept, the land was dry and filled with prickly pear cactus, scrub mesquite, armadillos, and rattlesnakes. Rugged plateaus, high escarpments, and dusty canyons marked the way to the dark mountains that clawed at the clouds.

The rolling hill country stretched southward with tall limestone cliffs above rivers lined with hardy cottonwood and cypress trees. Giant, sheltering oak trees, stands of pecan, and other types of trees grew more numerous closer to the Great Green Water. It was said that the Great Sky Spirit went to these shores when he was angry with his children. There, he would throw blinding, white fire into the sky, make the winds howl like a thousand wolves, and force the salty water to roll, pitch, and cover the land till his anger was spent. Such were the lands where the Great Sky Spirit's people lived.

After many cold seasons, the village had grown large, and the village's young leader, Chief Standing Bear, and his life-long friend, Red Bear, talked about whether the village should move to fresh northern lands, beyond the river. Standing Bear wanted the people to stay near the lake, the great forest, and the burial place of their ancestors. Red Bear, however, argued that the earth and the forest were growing tired of giving them food and that they should move before there was not enough food or room for the growing village. After many seasons of arguments between the two friends at the night fires, the village people had become divided, half behind each man.

One cool spring morning after yet another heated argument the night before, Red Bear angrily told his followers that they were leaving to search for a new place to build a village on the other side of the river, to the north. Furious, Standing Bear stood at the edge of the village and watched silently with a set jaw and crossed arms, as Red Bear and his followers prepared to leave the village. Gathering their belongings, recovering their lodge poles, and saying tearful farewells to friends and family, they set off to establish a new village on the river's far side.

It was a sad day for all, except the two impetuous friends, who had grown angry because their pride was bigger than their love for each other and for their people.

As Red Bear left the village, he could see his friend's stoic anger and swore on his infant son's life that his shadow would never share the same ground with his friend's shadow.

Watching his friend and his followers leave and hearing Red Bear's angry vow, Standing Bear also swore a vow that he too would never stand beside his friend again.

Their vows of separation were shouted for all their respective followers to hear, which made the division law. People in both villages knew it was now forbidden to ever seek out or speak with people from the village being established across the river.

Red Bear, now a chief, disappeared into the dark shadows of the forest trail, leading his followers to the land north of the river.

Standing Bear and his people watched their family and friends leave the old village. When the last member of the departing group disappeared into the woods, they went back to their daily lives with a heavy sadness in their hearts.

Many annual hunts passed, and both Standing Bear and Red Bear's villages flourished. Yet even with the passing of time, neither chief's pride softened. People from each village would occasionally see one another from across the river or would spot the other group of hunters traveling north to the annual buffalo hunt. But true to each chief's prideful vow, neither group ever openly acknowledged the other.

The Great Sky Spirit watched the effect that the two friends' stubborn pride had on his children and he was saddened by it. He hoped that they could find a way to soften their hearts and bring all his children back together somehow.

Long Feather stepped knee-deep into the cold water. Every week or so, she came here. Her toes flexed into the muddy sand, feeling for the hard river mussels. They tended to gather in the shallow pool beside the big rock that jutted out into the river from the shore. Feeling the round hardness of another mussel, she bent down, snagged it from the bottom, washed it clean of the muddy sand, and tossed it into the grass basket a few feet away on the shore.

She liked that no one else ever wanted to come with her to

walk in the river. It gave her time to be by herself and to enjoy the rushing of the river, the chirping birds, and the wind moving the leaves in the trees. Six moons earlier, she would have been poking sticks at fish or chasing tadpoles, but lately, those pursuits had seemed silly to her.

These days, she found herself thinking more about her mother, her father, and her future in the village. She had also noticed herself being more interested in what other villagers talked about and observing how they looked at each other. She also grew more aware of how things smelled. She could tell when a woman had bathed in the river and how older men smelled differently than younger men.

Long Feather's calves started to lose feeling in the cold water, so she decided it was time to gather her basket and head back to the village. River mussels were a favorite of her mother, Smiling Moon, and she was happy she would bring enough home for a good meal.

As she stepped onto the shore and picked up her basket of mussels, she caught movement out of the corner of her eye. She instantly crouched behind the large rock. A bear must be moving along the shallows, looking for fish. But a stealthy glance around the rock showed her that the movement was no bear.

Instead, what she saw made her duck back behind the rock again. She slowly shifted her position to hug the rock and slowly peek around it.

Across the river, a young brave stood on the opposite shore, looking up and down the river as if searching for something. Satisfied with no threats in sight, he untied his leggings and breechcloth and let them drop to the ground. Taking one more cautious look up and down the river, he stepped into the chilly shallows on his side of the river. He walked out until he was waist-deep in the water, seeming careful not to slip and fall. He cupped his hands together and threw water onto his head and face. He repeated the process multiple times.

Though he was farther than a stone's throw from Long Feather, she could make out his physique. He was lean, bare-chested, and tall with dark hair that hung to his shoulders. Try as she might, she couldn't make out the finer features of his face because of the distance. She watched him splash the water on himself and rub his face, neck, and skin above and below the water's surface. As she watched, she found herself both frightened and for some reason excited.

Soon, another young brave emerged from the forest and walked to the riverbank near where the bather stood in the water. He looked around and called out to the bather, obviously a companion. The bather turned and spoke to his friend while waving, encouraging him to get in the water. His companion shook his head while gesturing at the river, making it clear that he wanted nothing to do with getting in the river. It appeared that he was much more afraid of water demons than his friend.

The bather shook his head then dropped under the water for a moment before he rose back up and headed toward the shore. Water glistened as it streamed down his back. As the bather approached shore, still knee-deep in the river, his shore-bound companion yelled something, laughed, and pointed at him.

Obviously angry at what he heard from his friend, the bather yelled back something harsh, scooped up a rock from the river bottom, and threw it at his tormentor who leaped out of the way. Three steps later, the bather was on the shore, tying his leggings and breechcloth around his waist. Still dripping, he followed his laughing companion toward the forest.

But just before he stepped into the shadows, he turned and seemed to look directly at the rock which Long Feather was hiding behind.

She jerked her head back as her heart almost jumped out of her chest. She lay back on the rock while thinking about what she had just seen. Her heart pounded, and a warm feeling drifted across her neck and cheeks. She let out the breath she had been holding in a long sigh.

Laying on the sun-warmed rock, she waited for a time to make sure the two young braves had left the far riverside. Slowly, she rose from the rock and stepped away, catching her reflection in the still water beside her. It was smiling back at her, and the idea of coming to the river to dig for mussels seemed even more appealing than before.

Every few days through the early warm season, she returned to the same spot to dig mussels from the shallow water. Sometimes, she would hide if the same young brave came to wash, drink, or pull fish from the traps built among the partially submerged cypress roots. A couple of times, she openly walked, looking for mussels in the clear, shallow waters. She pretended not to notice him watching her from behind a tree or bush from across the river. Several times, she had even bathed near the rock, wondering if he was watching. But she kept her back to his riverside and acted as if she was totally alone. These days, she wanted to be seen by the young brave, but she wasn't exactly sure why.

The days had grown warmer and then hotter and longer in Long Feather's world. She found herself spending more time near the cooking fire and watching her mother work. She made small tender bundles for restarting fires and gathered wood from the forest. She even found herself listening more to the gossip and stories the village women told as they went about their daily tasks.

Smiling Moon had noticed her daughter's change of interests and brought her along to work on tasks with other women. She always kept her within view, so she could see her reactions to what the other women talked about.

Long Feather learned how to plant, how to shell and grind corn, and how to prepare fish, meat, and berries for drying. She learned how to plant and pick cotton, pick out the seeds, and twist the remaining fibers into longer strands for weaving blankets and clothes. At her mother's encouragement and with help from the other women, Long Feather made a cotton blanket. She was told that soon it might be her joining blanket.

Sometimes, she sat with the other women while they talked and chewed deer hide strips until they were soft enough to use as carrying and binding straps. While working they would sometimes ask her if she had noticed some of the young village braves looking at her and if she liked any of them. At hearing the question, she would blush, shake her head, and look away. She worked hard and learned many new skills from the village women, but she always made sure she had time to dig for mussels.

More often now, she and the young brave at the river would watch each other openly as they went about their individual tasks. It was as if they knew each other and were working together, but they never actually acknowledged the other. She found herself thinking more about the young brave from across the river and hoped he was thinking about her.

Like Long Feather's mother, her father, Standing Bear, had also taken to watching her more closely when he was near her in the village. Long Feather had noticed her father's attention and how he would occasionally whisper to her mother and the other women who spent time with her. She knew they talked about her because they would look in her direction and sometimes nod as if agreeing on something.

She had also noticed that it was different when he or her mother spoke to her now. If she didn't respond quickly or if she smiled too much, they would be cross with her and tell her that she was no longer a child. She needed to be more serious. But whenever she felt tired from her new chores or irritated at her parents, she would think of the young brave at the river and a smile would leap to her face.

One warm evening when she and her mother were about to finish preparing their evening meal, her father and a young brave named One Green Eye walked toward their cooking fire. Though older now, Long Feather immediately recognized him.

Standing Bear spoke as they approached. "Wife, daughter. I have invited One Green Eye to share our food. Make a place for him, daughter. I have told him that you are a good cook, and he wishes to taste this for himself."

One Green Eye watched Long Feather through hard, appraising eyes. Doing as her father had told her, she set a skin-covered rest near her father's rest by the fire and returned to help her mother fill the food bowls.

Once seated, her father and One Green Eye took what they wanted from the bowls, leaving the rest for Long Feather and her mother to share. During the meal, One Green Eye watched Long Feather eat as he and Standing Bear talked of the annual buffalo hunt that would be coming soon.

Near the end of the meal, Standing Bear held up his bowl and spoke to One Green Eye. "I told you she was a good cook."

One Green Eye, who was three hunts older than Long

Feather, grunted. "I have been told she is good at finding mussels in the river." He looked at her and she averted her eyes to her food bowl. "Mussels are for women and old men with bad teeth. My woman would not spend her time playing in the river like an otter." He kept staring at her as he continued. "She would stay in the village, bear me fat sons, keep my firewood pile high, clean my lodge, and cook the deer I kill, which is what strong braves eat."

Long Feather's eyes flashed with anger as she realized the meaning of One Green Eye's visit to their fire. Before showing her anger, she got up and took the empty food bowls to the fire. She wiped them clean with grass while getting angrier with every stroke. She now understood why she had been working with the village women. She was now seen as a woman and a potential wife. She knew she was bound to her father's word, and if he bargained her marriage to One Green Eye, her fate would be sealed.

She fumed at the prospect of being One Green Eye's wife.

Days passed without any word of One Green Eye being spoken by her mother or father. She hoped One Green Eye had found her undesirable as a wife. But she noticed that he made a point of being more noticeable anywhere she might be working in the village. Anytime she looked toward him, he looked at her with his cruel smile that she remembered from when they were both children.

She had known him since she was young, and those memories weren't any she cherished. It was common knowledge that One Green Eye's father had often beat his wife to the point where her father had been forced to speak with him as the village chief. One Green Eye's mother had been a gentle woman who died giving him life. His father refused him from birth, so he was raised by the families in the village. His father had died in the annual hunt soon after his birth and was not grieved by the people of the village.

One Green Eye had been born with one green eye and one brown eye, which was likely why his father didn't want him. He might've thought he was somehow cursed. The village women whispered that the mark proved that two wolves lived inside him: one good like his mother and one bad like his father. Long Feather didn't know about a good wolf living in him, but she was sure a bad one was there. She wondered if the good wolf had lost the fight for his spirit and had been eaten by the bad wolf.

When they were children, One Green Eye had always enjoyed teasing or bullying the younger children including Long Feather. Any chance he had to push her down or trip her when they were running was never missed. He would always stand over her and laugh as she laid in the dirt.

After Long Feather had complained to her mother about him, Smiling Moon had explained that he teased her because he liked her. Long Feather had never believed she spoke true. If he did like her, she wished he wouldn't *like* her so much. Several times, she had seen him put blackthorn twigs on a well-used trail or hide stinkwood in firewood piles. She had even found him hitting the village dogs with sticks, just for fun. The last time she had caught him at it, he was beating a runt pup with a stick and laughing every time the dog yelped in pain. Trying to stop him, she had pleaded with him.

"So, Long Feather, you want me to train you instead?" he had asked, turning his attention to her and laughing with that cruel smile. "I will enjoy doing that." He had walked toward her while brandishing the stick.

"I am no runt pup, One Green Eye," she had warned, preparing to protect herself from his blows. "You will not find me as easy to beat."

After enduring several painful whacks on her upheld arms, she had grabbed his stick, jerking it from his hand. She had hit him back with the stick several times as other children watched and laughed. One Green Eye had run away toward the quiet safety of the forest, but not before giving her a look of pure hatred.

She still occasionally saw him around the village as they grew up, but he always seemed to make a point to stay a good distance from her. He still teased, bullied, and did mischief, but he made himself scarce when he saw her.

Now years later, the thought of being his wife and being expected to cow to his word made her face burn with anger. "You may not find me any easier to train as a wife," she hissed under her breath.

Hot days turned more temperate, and the nights cooled as the village chores changed in preparation for the colder season ahead. Long Feather's mother told her to finish her joining blanket because One Green Eye might bargain with her father for her to be his wife soon. This comment angered her, but she held her tongue. She wanted to be a good, obedient daughter, but the thought of One Green Eye's cold smile while he touched her made her skin crawl. Her mother and father seemed happy she was working on the joining blanket, and her father even gave her a small basket of blueberries to make blue dye. There hadn't been enough berries, so she could only dye most of the blanket, leaving some of it white. But there was still time to get more blueberries. Or so she hoped.

On her next trip to the river, the young brave on the other side waved when Long Feather appeared.

Startled and looking around first to assure they were alone, she hand-talked to him. "Why you wave? Forget law?"

The young brave abruptly stopped waving, taken aback. Women were not supposed to know hand-talk since it was how the braves communicated during hunting, across distances, or to unknown braves they met when traveling. After several moments, his surprise gave way to curiosity. "Who are you?" he hand-talked, blatantly ignoring the no contact law. "How you hand-talk?"

"I Long Feather," she replied. "I watch Father teach young braves hand-talk. Who are you?"

"I Blue Stone, son to Chief Red Bear," he hand-talked and then noticed Long Feather's shoulders had dropped at his response to her question.

After a moment, she hand-talked, "I Long Feather…" She paused too long. "I daughter to Chief Standing Bear."

Blue Stone instantly understood her sadness as his heart also sank. He remembered the old feud and both their fathers' vows of separation.

For a few moments, they both stood there looking at each other, unmoving. Each felt the weight of realization that it was much more than just a river that separated them. Slowly, without any more hand-talk, they both turned away, leaving the cold, uncaring river to flow between them.

⋘⋙

Lodge repair, wood gathering, food drying, and blanket making became important work for the women as the men knapped flint and dried sinew for spear tips. Most men were preparing for the annual buffalo hunt on the northern plains. Meat, hides, horns, and bone would be taken to fill the village's needs during the cold time to come. Soon The Great Sky Spirit would no longer be able to keep the howling Blue Wolf locked away in the north's great cave. When he came to their land, he would bring the cold, bitter winds and death would often follow.

The cooler winds made the river too cold for digging muscles, so Long Feather had taken to gathering winter firewood in the woods near the big rock along the river trail. She had wrapped the unfinished blue and white joining blanket around her shoulders to protect her from the morning chill. The blanket's blue was a shade darker than the sky, and the white portion matched the white, puffy clouds.

Over the last weeks, Long Feather and Blue Stone had paused to silently watch each other on occasions when they were both at the river. He had unenthusiastically waved at her on several occasions, and she had parroted the motion back at him. The waving only made them both feel sadder, and neither had hand-talked since the day they had shared their names. But each had made sure they were alone before waving as they knew their villages were still bound by their fathers' vows. There was nothing that would change those vows either.

A week later, Long Feather walked toward the river to gather firewood. Her chores had kept her away from the river longer than usual. She hoped she would see Blue Stone, but worried he might have given up on her, which might be for the better. Upon arriving at the shore, she looked around and across the river, but she could see no one. Her heart sank.

After a few moments though, Blue Stone stepped out of the forest's shadows on the other side. He wore a deerskin, long-sleeve shirt. They both looked up and down their river-side before they waved to each other.

Hearing a rustle of branches in the woods behind her, she ducked and snuck a short distance back up the river trail to see if someone was coming to the river. The sun was low, and the trail was in deep shadow. Standing still and watching for a short time, she saw no movement nor heard anyone approaching, so she turned back to the shore and Blue Stone.

As she approached the riverbank, he raised up from behind some grass, and for a moment, their eyes almost seemed to meet. The wind didn't feel as cool as it had before.

"I soon go hunt," Blue Stone hand-talked.

Long Feather thought about her village's men preparing for the annual hunt in the north as well. She also imagined One Green Eye's leering smile and felt the weight of the unfinished joining blanket around her shoulders. She took a deep breath. "Blue Stone… I pledged to marriage soon," she hand-talked. "I marry man I hate." Her heart broke, but she felt that she owed Blue Stone the truth about her situation. "My father soon make pledge. I am bound."

Blue Stone was shaken by what she told him and looked up into the sky as if looking for the Great Sky Spirit that lived there. It was several long moments before he brought his eyes back to her. "If could, would you be my woman?"

Her heart jumped in her chest, but she calmed herself before answering. "The law?" she asked. "It cannot be. You are cruel."

"Father's pride is not law. That truth?" He looked eagerly at her.

She solemnly signed, "Your words are true. Pride not law."

He looked down. His head moved side to side in obvious frustration. Finally, he looked up and fixed his eyes on her.

"You be my woman." He hesitated before continuing. "I break law. I come to you. I take you toward Great Green Water to live."

Long Feather's heart soared, and she smiled. "I break law also. I be your woman."

Blue Stone beamed and thought a few moments before hand-talking. "I return from hunt. I come here dawn after full moon. I see your blanket, I come, we go away. I not see blanket…" He paused for a moment considering. "I not come this place forever." With that, he held up his hand in a solemn wave to her for several moments, turned, and walked back into the woods.

For a few minutes, she stood there, holding the memory of his words in her mind. This was a chance for a happy life, or at least the chance of a life without being with One Green Eye. She could feel the leaf-filtered sunlight on her face. The hissing of the wind pushing through the treetops and the gurgle of the moving water all sounded different from what she remembered before this moment. She knew that everything she loved about her world would be nothing without Blue Stone. Just the thought of never seeing him again made her knees weak, her stomach ache, and her eyes burn. She couldn't let that happen. She turned, picking up her wood bundle, and walked back toward the village while deep in thought about what she had to do.

She never saw One Green Eye as he stepped out of the shadowed woods near the riverbank. His face burned hot as he thought about Blue Stone and his promise to meet Long Feather here and run away with her. He vowed that Blue Stone would never touch what was rightfully his.

The first day of the annual hunt came at sunrise two mornings later. The village men packed before dawn, and at first light, they began their trek toward the northern plains. Each man carried a traveling bundle on his back, and excited dogs, dragging skid litters of supplies, yelped excitedly as they left the village. The hunting party would travel east along the long lake trail to where it ended and then turn north toward the rolling grass prairie. That was where the great buffalo herd would soon arrive for winter.

All the women, older men, and children stood at the edge of the village and watched the procession. Soon, all had disappeared into the woods, and those remaining began their daily chores and the weeks of waiting for the hunters to return. Only village sounds could be heard. Long Feather went about her chores, glad that One Green Eye had also left on the hunt.

The village was much quieter, and those left behind went about preparing for the coming cold season and the returning hunters. Clay pots were filled with corn and dry fish. High frames were built to hang, scrape and dry the great hides, and litters of green branches were built near firepits to dry the salted buffalo meat. Deerskin clothes were mended with dry sinew, and new jackets were made.

All the while, Long Feather watched the moon change phases and thought about One Green Eye and her father but mostly Blue Stone's last words to her.

Many days passed, and after a while, the old men sat at the village's north edge. They looked across the lake and toward the distant hills searching for the first sign that the hunting party was nearing home.

Long Feather had watched the moon appear and grow to almost full over time and had decided what she would do the morning after the full moon.

Late one evening as the old men stared across the lake, four tiny yellow dots of light appeared to the north as darkness fell. They shared concerned looks. Those were signal fires from the returning hunting party, who had camped on the far hills one last night before reaching home. The signal fires told of the hunt's success and prepared the village for news of lost braves.

After a time of watching the four fires, no more fires were added, and none were extinguished. The old men smiled and sang songs about how the Great Sky Spirit had protected them from harm and had brought them to this land. Four fires meant lots of buffalo had been taken, and any killed braves would have been indicated by the number of extinguished fires.

The women had anxiously noted the four specks of light in the distance and relaxed when they heard the old men's laughter and songs. The coming winter would be easier with lots of food and no lost husbands or sons to grieve for. The good news spread through the village, and everyone excitedly anticipated the hunters return home by the next evening.

The sun was low the next day when the hunting party emerged from the forest. The returning men yelled greetings and the dogs barked, announcing their arrival. The men carried bigger bundles than when they had left, and their dogs dragged sleds with poles bowed under the weight of meat and hides. The hunt had indeed been a good one.

The women and children ran to meet fathers, sons, and brothers and to help carry the heavy bundles and sleds back into the waiting village. Husbands and wives embraced, and stories of the hunt were shared as the old men questioned the hunters as they came to sit by cooking fires.

Long Feather's father touched his forehead to her mother's, and they both smiled and embraced. Standing Bear looked at

Long Feather through tired eyes and smiled a happy greeting at her. The greeting had always made her feel warm and happy in the past, but now she turned away and pretended to work on something by the fire. As her anticipation of seeing Blue Stone grew, her sadness at knowing what her actions would do to her father also grew.

Fires were built up, and the women roasted the salted buffalo meat that was recovered from bundles. Flat rocks were heated on which to cook honey corn cakes, and the whole village settled into celebrating the successful hunt.

Long Feather was helping other women serve when One Green Eye spotted her from another cooking fire and strode toward her. One hand was behind his back. "Long Feather," he called out.

Her father watched him approach.

"Long Feather, I have brought you a gift from the hunt." As she stood to face him, he stopped before her, held out a large, shiny, black horn, and smiled.

Her father and mother were now both watching the exchange.

"This horn," he said, holding it above his head for all to see, "is from the largest beast killed on the hunt, and I killed it. It will make many weaving needles, necklaces, and sharp awls to pierce skins for sewing my son's clothes." He looked around, speaking louder. "I hope you finished your joining blanket, Long Feather. During the hunt, your father pledged you to be my wife, and I want to bargain for his blessing and have the joining ceremony as soon as possible."

Her heart stopped. Everyone nearby was looking at her and One Green Eye. She wanted to run out of the village and never stop running, but her memory of Blue Stone smiling and his words of hope kept her standing where she was.

Forcing a tight smile, she turned to One Green Eye and spoke in an equally loud voice. "One Green Eye... Our village—and probably the village to the north—has heard what your intentions are toward me."

Several people, including her nearby parents, smiled at her words.

"Tonight is a celebration of a good hunt, of our hunters' skills, and for the knowledge that the cold season to come will not be lean and hungry. For us to celebrate a marriage blessing now would make the hunt's celebration small. Why not wait till after the full moon and give our village another night of celebration to look forward to?" She tilted her head, looking at him with a wry smile. "Surely another few days' wait will not soften your..." She paused, making an exaggerated stare at his waist. "...intentions for me."

With that said, everyone laughed and nodded to one another with raised eyebrows and shared whispers.

One Green Eye's smile faded as he looked around and realized he had been made the butt of a joke. Turning back to Long Feather, he locked eyes with hers as he spoke. "You are truly wise Long Feather." He forced a tight smile. "Two celebrations are much better than one. I still have to bargain with your father on the price for his blessing, so waiting a few days more will be a good thing." He then leaned close to her ear so only she could hear him. "I look forward to dulling your sharp tongue and keeping your belly fat with many sons. You will soon be *my* woman like *my* lodge, *my* dogs, and everything I own."

She snapped her head back to look at him with fiery eyes.

He backed away from her with an exaggerated, leering smile meant for the crowd. "She whispers that she is eager to know my intentions!" He said, thrusting his midsection briefly and joining the laughter that erupted around him. Waving the shiny black buffalo horn, he walked away to join several other braves moving toward another fire. He cast a hard glance back at her over his shoulder.

She felt a coldness deeper than the waters of the nearby river grip her.

The next morning, Long Feather arose just before the sun, left the lodge, and busied herself with rekindling the cooking fire from the gray ashes. She had slept badly, dreaming that she was a small child again while One Green Eye was a grown man. In the dream, she had a strap around her neck that was tied to a lodge pole, and he would laugh while hitting her with a stick every time she tried to speak.

She focused on formulating her departure plan and how to prepare.

Her mother emerged from the lodge. She knelt beside Long Feather, watching her out of the corner of her eyes as she made breakfast. She spoke offhandedly without looking at her daughter. "When I was your age, I found out my father had pledged me to be the wife of Standing Bear. I was so scared that I even thought of running away."

Long Feather kept breaking tinder but turned her head toward her mother slightly.

"Your father was big and loud. He only seemed to care for himself and what he could do. He never seemed interested in me. He ignored me when we shared food at our family's fire or when he would sit and speak with my father. This only made me even more scared of what being his wife would be like. But, as always, I obeyed my father. I made my joining blanket, and after the joining ceremony, I went to Standing Bear's lodge to be his wife."

Long Feather now looked at her mother with hard, questioning eyes. She had only known her father to be a gentle man who rarely raised his voice. He had shown her and her mother nothing but loving kindness. How could the man in her mother's story be the gentle father she knew? She asked as much to her mother with a disbelieving look and a shake of her head.

Her mother kept talking as she pressed a ball of rough cornmeal on a hot stone and scraped another hand full of wet cornmeal from a clay pot. "We went to his lodge that night after the joining ceremony. As is the custom, everyone followed us to sit outside our lodge, singing and yelling taunts at us. I had been there earlier that day to bring my possessions and to prepare the marriage pallet with my joining blanket. As we knelt there facing each other, your father reached for me, but I stopped him. I told him that before lying together, I needed to teach him the Water-Hand game."

Smiling Moon paused for a moment to let her daughter's curiosity build and to slap the next corn cake on the hot, flat stone.

"Of course Standing Bear looked at me curiously, but he sat back and listened. Kneeling in front of him, I reached forward, took both of his hands, and placed them side by side with his cupped palms facing up. I picked up a drinking gourd and poured water into his hands. I told him to close his hands and use all his great strength to hold as much water as he could. He did as I asked, closing his hands into tight fists. After a moment, I told him to open his hands and show me how much water he had captured."

Long Feather wrinkled her brow, as if trying to understand the point of the game.

Her mother continued as she made the next corn cake. "Your father smiled like I was a silly child, but he opened his fists and showed me his damp, empty hands. 'Smiling Moon,' he said, 'even if I use all my strength to hold the water, it will always slip between my fingers.'

"That's when I leaned in close, looked into his eyes, and whispered, 'Standing Bear, my husband, what I say now is a truth as cold and hard as a stone from the river. I am like the water. Try to use your strength to hold me, and I *will* slip away through your fingers. But use wisdom and gentleness to make a place for me in your heart, and I will always be here to keep your belly full, your pallet warm and see to it that you are happy long after your great strength has left you."

Long Feather tilted her head at her mother. "And what did your new husband say to that?"

Smiling Moon was quiet for a few moments as she turned the corn cakes over to brown on the other side. She looked at her daughter with one eyebrow up and a corner of her mouth slightly lifted. "Well…as you have said, you have only known your father to be a wise and gentle man." Her smile grew fuller as she turned to look down at the cake she removed from the rock. "And I still share his pallet."

With that, both women laughed heartily as they turned their attention back to preparing the meal.

But even though her mother had lifted her spirits, Long Feather knew that One Green Eye had little, if any, wisdom and no gentleness within him that she could ever bring out. "I don't think One Green Eye would see the lesson of the Water-Hand game," she said, looking into her mother's eyes. "He boasts too loud, he beats his dogs for no reason, and when he looks at me, I feel only coldness."

Her mother looked down as if searching for something

to say that would ease her daughter's worried mind. After a moment, she looked back up with a forced smile and spoke evenly. "Sometimes even the hardest lump of clay can be softened with time and then worked into a useful—"

"One Green Eye is not clay, and he has no goodness in him. I fear that if I am his wife, he will beat me and turn me into something ugly, worn, and sad of heart," she finished with tears glistening in her eyes. She knew then that there was no way to avoid her fate as One Green Eye's wife if she stayed in the village.

She went silent, avoiding her mother's occasional sideways glance, and helped her finish preparing breakfast. Her mind drifted back to planning to run away with Blue Stone. She only knew him by the months of watching him and his hand-talked words. She admitted that she did not know if he loved her or that she truly loved him. But she did know that her heart soared with excitement when she thought of him or when he looked at her as they waved or hand-talked across the river. She also knew in her heart that even if Blue Stone wasn't as good a man as she felt he was, he could never be as bad as One Green Eye.

The day started like most others except that those who had stayed up telling hunting stories arrived late to the morning fires only to find their corn cakes cold, overcooked, and dry. Wives working the nearby hide frames watched their husbands with stern eyes, daring them to complain about the cold, hard food. The village dogs ate well that morning. By midday, Long Feather was at the frames, scraping buffalo hides with the village women. Others boiled the bones for marrow and used razor-sharp pieces of flint to cut raw buffalo meat into thin strips for soaking in salt water before laying them on smaller green-stick racks near low fires to dry into jerky.

Long Feather was glad that the hunters' return was so close to her departure as it would keep everyone busy and assure all slept heavily for the next few nights. It would make it easier to slip out of the village the sunrise after next to meet Blue Stone by the river.

She visualized what would happen after her departure that morning. When her mother would awaken, she would find Long Feather and her belongings gone and would know she had run away rather than marry One Green Eye. Her mother would dutifully awaken Standing Bear and tell him what had happened. Soon, the whole village would know Long Feather had disobeyed her father and run away.

Her father would rightfully be angry and ashamed of her. He would make a great show of breaking her eating bowl and throwing it into the cooking fire to show all that she was now considered dead to him. Her mother would hide in their lodge, wailing, pulling out her hair, and scratching her arms and face with sticks and thorns to mark her sadness for the "death" of her runaway daughter.

Her eyes filled with tears, and her stomach churned at the thought of what her running away would do to her parents. But she knew she could never convince herself that she could be with One Green Eye. At least no one would ever know she had run away with Blue Stone, so an already bad situation would not be compounded by the knowledge she had also broken the village's law. All would eventually assume she had fallen victim to the elements or hungry animals, and after a while, the village and her parents would return to normal life.

She didn't know what her future with Blue Stone would hold as they traveled south, putting distance between them and their villages. But she did know that the feelings she had for him would grow stronger when she could finally feel his touch on her skin. For a while, the traveling would be rough, walking from sunrise to sunset, eating berries and nuts on the move, and sleeping on the ground together, wrapped in her joining blanket. After many days of traveling, Blue Stone would look for a safe place to make their solitary home. Outcasts from both villages.

Her heart beat with excitement as she envisioned Blue Stone standing on the other side of the swift river, scanning the other shore. He'd squint through the early dawn, trying to find the big rock and hoping to see her standing there wrapped in the blue and white joining blanket, the sign that she would go with him as his woman.

Long Feather became aware that several women at other drying racks nearby were looking quizzically at her and realized she was no longer scraping the hide. Apparently, she had been standing there frozen in thoughts of life with Blue Stone, likely with a childish grin on her face. Recovering her senses, she said something to the effect of, "I was thinking of my joining night with One Green Eye." The women smiled, nodded their heads knowingly, and whispered to each other. Long Feather hated lying but she couldn't tell the truth. She refocused and went back to scraping the hide until it was time to go to their cooking fire and begin supper.

Smiling Moon was already cracking nuts for roasting. Long Feather met her mother's eyes as she jerked her head toward the dwindling wood pile. Without losing a step, she scooped up the kindling strap and kept walking past the fire. She headed toward the woods on the other side of the village.

There had been some strong winds that day which meant lots of deadfall in the woods. Covering the distance quickly, she smiled as she saw dead branches on the ground. Picking them up, she crept along while filling her arm.

She jumped with a start when a thick branch cracked just ahead of her. Looking up, she saw One Green Eye step out from behind a tree, holding a long branch and smiling at her.

"Getting ready to beat your dog One Green Eye?" she asked sarcastically while breaking another long branch into shorter pieces.

His smile enlarged, but his eyes were not smiling. "Maybe I'm picking out a sturdy one to beat you with on our joining night. As I am told, you were caught dreaming about that at the hide racks today."

Her face burned at the thought of the wagging village tongues spreading her earlier lie. But then…it suddenly came to her that her lie could actually be used to her advantage for running away the morning after the full moon. She forced a change in her demeanor before speaking. "What can I say?" She gulped hard. "I've begun to see the wisdom in being your… wife." The word stuck like bile in her throat for a moment before she forced it out. "You're a great hunter, as proven by the beautiful black horn you offered me and the hides you bring to the racks. Also, your strength, speed, and wisdom are known to all…that will listen." Her stomach rolled as she forced herself to continue. "What woman could continue to deny what is so plain to all? I was silly to turn away your attention. One Green Eye, I ask you go to my father and bargain for his blessing, so our joining day can be set for a time soon after the coming full moon."

His eyes narrowed and his face froze in obvious confusion. He seemed to think hard for a few moments on what she had just said. Reaching some conclusion, his face split into a wide, prideful smile, and he stepped forward, tossing the branch at her ankles. "You see…" He gestured toward the stick he threw. "I will be a good husband and helpful to you." With that, he let out a whoop. He almost knocked her to the ground as he brushed past her, rushing back toward the village.

She watched him go, knowing he would soon be bragging to the other men about his conquest of her. No doubt before the last fire died out tonight, most of the village, including her parents, would think she had given in to marrying him. And with any luck, a bargain would be struck between One Green Eye and her father by tomorrow evening. Fueling the farce to her advantage even more.

Long Feather had an idea of how to turn her runaway departure into something less damning. This new "giving in to joining" strategy would work to her advantage. It would make a story of leaving to forage for blueberry skins the morning after the full moon to finish dying her joining blanket very believable. Everyone would just think she was working hard to finish her joining blanket quickly. Her failure to return from "foraging" that evening would lead everyone to believe she had been snatched by a water demon or forest spirit. The village men, likely led by her father, would spend the day after her disappearance looking for her around the berry thicket at the far end of the lake trail. And finding no traces of her there would only add to the belief that a spirit or demon was responsible for her disappearance. No one would ever suspect she and Blue Stone were actually well on their way to a new life together.

Thinking more about it, she knew this meant she could only take her joining blanket and a basket for "blueberry skins." But if leaving her few other possessions behind would solidify the belief that she was dead, all the better. She would be long gone with Blue Stone and free of One Green Eye forever. Her father and mother would only face the sorrow of a daughter's death instead of the shame of her defying them and running away. She felt rather proud of her plan but sad at the same time.

A short time later, she returned to the village with her wood bundle tied up on her back. Weaving her way through the evening cook fires and lodges, she noticed a few women smiling at her. In fact, as she got deeper into the village, several women stopped their work to smile at her. She knew One Green Eye had definitely been busy bragging about winning her over.

She chuckled softly to herself, apparently the three fastest ways of spreading gossip in her village was by hand-talk, fire signal, and telling One Green Eye.

"Well," she thought while taking a deep breath, "I am truly committed to my plan now." A small knot of fear formed in the pit of her stomach.

As Long Feather approached her mother's fire, her mother looked up, saw her, and hugged her with tears in her eyes and a happy smile. "I just heard the good news, daughter," she said, holding her at arm's length and looking at her as if it was the first time. "You've made your father and me very happy and proud." She helped her daughter set the bundle of limbs on the wood pile. "And I know that One Green Eye will be a better husband than you think he will," she added, rubbing her daughter's upper arms with a half smile and sad eyes.

Hearing her mother's warm words and feeling her loving touch didn't make Long Feather feel better. Instead, she could only visualize her mother's scratched and bloody face to the news of her missing and presumed dead daughter. The vision only brought tears to her eyes. Such a cruel lie that she was about to place upon her parents. Was it really any better than the truth? She knew in her heart it was better, if only a little.

Seeing her daughter standing still, arms hanging limp at her sides, with tears streaming down her cheeks made Smiling Moon wrap her arm around her waist and pull her to kneel next to her by the fire. She wiped the tears from her cheeks, took her hands in hers, and leaned in close. "I know the thought of being bound to a husband and making a new life with him is scary to think about." She smiled at her daughter as she gave her another brief hug around her shoulders. "But you will have many good moments to hold in your heart as well." With that, she released her daughter and began sifting the ashes with a stick, looking for the morning fire's embers that were deep under the gray ash.

Long Feather smiled at her mother's words. Those were indeed the thoughts and fears that had been going through her mind, but those feelings didn't involve One Green Eye at all—rather Blue Stone.

She went to the wood bundle, untied it, and broke off some small, dry twigs before moving back to help. As she and her mother got the fire going again and began making the meal, her mother shared woman talk with her daughter while they worked. Occasionally, she looked at her mother in open mouth disbelief, while at other times she looked down with reddened cheeks, nodding. By the time Standing Bear arrived to eat, she was more frightened and confused about marriage than she had been before talking to her mother.

Seeing the confusion on her daughter's face, Smiling Moon reached over and patted her daughter's hand. "Don't think about it too much. It will all seem right at the right time."

With that, they passed food to Standing Bear who had seated himself near the fire. He observed the two women with suspicious eyes. The meal was silent with him watching them eat and make a point not to look in his direction. As they finished the meal, her mother built up the fire while she scraped the remnants of food from the eating bowls into it.

The deafening silence was too great for him. "So, I am told that One Green Eye has decided to take a wife and she has agreed." He said it sarcastically, eying his wife and daughter as they busied themselves.

Neither reacted to his words.

"Am I to be told about this by my family, or do I act surprised when One Green Eye boasts about it when he comes to bargain for my blessing?" He had obvious frustration in his voice and on his face.

Long Feather broke the silence as she approached and kneeled, facing her father, who looked at her with wide-eyed expectation. "It is true, Father. One Green Eye came to me when I was gathering firewood this afternoon. He again asked me to be his wife and share his lodge. We talked, and as I heard him, I thought of your wise words. He is a strong brave, a good hunter, and will provide many strong children to add strength to our village." Her face was downcast as she spoke. "He will come to bargain for your blessing. I ask only that you make him pay a good price." She started to rise but paused when a second thought came to her, so she added, "He also bragged that he would out bargain you because he was younger and smarter." She finished the lie and smiled inside. No reason that this should be easy or painless for One Green Eye.

She looked over to see her father's eyes flash with anger in the firelight.

Standing Bear snorted. "He may well be younger but

smarter…" He hesitated before turning his attention back to his daughter. His eyes softened as he spoke to her. "It is good that you are choosing to join with One Green Eye, daughter. Smiling Moon and I grow impatient for grandchildren to play at our lodge and listen to my stories. I believe One Green Eye will find the sharpness of your tongue, the strength of your spirit, and the cleverness of your mind to be more than a match." He reached out and patted Long Feather's hand gently. "Rest well tonight and worry no more. Finish your joining blanket and listen to the women and your mother as they prepare you for joining in the days to come." With that said, he leaned back against his rest and stared into the fire with a slight smirk on his face.

She stood up and told her parents that she was going to sleep. She hoped the Great Sky Spirit would understand her reason for lying to her parents and protect her from bad dreams of One Green Eye.

Watching her father and mother by the fire the next morning made Long Feather sad. This would be the last morning she would ever spend with them. She tried to burn every line and curve of their faces, the colors of their eyes, and the sounds of their voices into her memory. The odors of wood smoke, burned corn, and hot stones that she knew so well hung in the air around her. On the occasional light breeze that brushed her face were the smells of buffalo hides, dried grass, and the old dust of her village.

Looking around the village, she took in the sight of children playing among the lodges and men leaving the morning fires, heading to the many tasks to be done before the cold time came. She thought of Blue Stone and wondered if he was sitting at his fire, taking in his last morning before his world would fade behind him.

Long Feather's father jarred her from her thoughts. "Daughter." He spoke in his soft voice that was reserved for times around the fire with his family. "Now that you are promised to One Green Eye, do you have a time for the joining in your mind? I've seen that you have to finish dying your joining blanket. Tonight is the full moon, and the first hard winds of the cold time are not far away."

She saw her opportunity to set her plan in motion. She spoke casually as if she was completely resolved to the joining situation. "I'm planning to leave at sunrise in the morning and go to the blueberry thicket at the end of the lake trail. There may be enough berry skins left to gather and finish dying my blanket. Once that is done, it will be One Green Eye who decides when he wants the joining to take place." Her mind wandered once again to the image of Blue Stone standing in the water waving to her.

Her father nodded and smiled as he poked a stick at the coals of the morning fire. "You make my heart glad, daughter. I can hear your children's laughter in the night wind and see their happy faces when I close my eyes to sleep. I know your choice also pleases the Great Sky Spirit, and he will bless you and One Green Eye with a good life and many strong children."

Smiling Moon listened to the conversation and gave Long Feather a curious look but said nothing. She knew no blueberries were left so late in the season, but she would give her daughter the berry basket and some corn cakes to make her trip in the morning. It would give her some time by herself to think about the joining and her future. In her heart, she felt that tonight's full moon would mark her daughter's new place as a woman in the village.

Long Feather helped her mother clean up the morning meal and prepare for another day of work in the village as she always did. She knew that wherever she chose to work, her joining with One Green Eye would be the talk, and she readied herself to smile and to talk about it as if it were actually true.

One more night. Then she and Blue Stone would finally meet face-to-face and run away together. Again, her heart ached, knowing she would never see her mother and father again, but it also soared with the knowledge that she would never see One Green Eye again. She would never hear his boastful words, see his sneering smile, or feel his rough touch on her skin as his wife. And that thought made the false smile much easier.

That day, village life was as normal as it ever was. Children ran happily through the village to be shooed away by adults. Dogs barked, people talked, and everyone went about their everyday lives. Men left to hunt deer, catch fish, work on mending lodges, or see to a dozen other tasks to prepare for the cold time ahead. Women scraped animal hides, ground corn to store in clay jars, and saw to a hundred other tasks necessary to make life bearable during the cold time. Except for the honored old men and small children, everyone worked to earn a bowl of food at the fire and a warm pallet in the lodges.

The day proved as routine as any other. Long Feather scraped skins, gathered firewood, or jerked buffalo meat. Occasionally, she would feel One Green Eye's gaze and turn to spot him watching her from between lodges or while squatting at another fire. When she did, she summoned all her strength to force a coy smile and play the shy wife to be, so all would believe the lie. He would return her smile and turn away to busy himself elsewhere, no doubt preparing for his bargaining time with her father later that evening. As the sun got low in the sky, she headed back to her parent's lodge for her last evening meal with her parents.

As the evening meal finished up, Long Feather worked at building up the fire. She reminded her parents of her plan to rise early the next morning and spend the day gathering berry skins to finish dying her joining blanket. Her father offered to travel with her, but she told him that she wanted time to herself to think about all that was happening. She assured him that she would be back before the evening meal. She lied again.

He agreed but warned her to stay clear of the lake's deep parts that were near the trail. The water demons that lived in the deep water grabbed careless people and took them into the depths where they would never be seen again. She promised him that she would take care and keep a watchful eye for the water demons when she drank from the lake.

Right on schedule, a bustle of male voices approached Standing Bear's fire from between the lodges. He maintained his emotionless stare into the fire as if he hadn't noticed their approach. The men, led by One Green Eye, stopped across the fire from him.

Stepping forward from the group, One Green Eye planted his feet shoulder-width apart with his arms crossed and looked directly into Standing Bear's impassive face. When he spoke, it was stern and direct. "It is I, One Green Eye. I am here to bargain for your blessing to take Long Feather as my wife, as you have granted and she has agreed."

Slow moments passed by as no immediate reply came from Standing Bear, who sat unmoving staring into the fire. Eventually, he spoke, looking up into the young man's one green eye. "It is good you arrived when you did One Green Eye. Since I am old and weak-minded, I was just about to make water and then have my wife and daughter help me to an early sleep."

Hearing the overly sarcastic statement, One Green Eye shot a quick, hard glance at Long Feather, who stood by the nearby lodge. She was partially hidden behind her mother peeking out with a slight smile on her face.

Hiding his irritation at Standing Bear's carefully chosen words and tone, he spoke again. "You are a strong and wise chief, Standing Bear, and anyone who says you are not is not worth being heard." He cast another quick look at her.

Standing Bear smiled as he spoke. "Then sit as an equal at my fire, One Green Eye, and we shall bargain to see what people who speak such words are truly worth." With that, he gruffly addressed Smiling Moon and Long Feather standing by the lodge. "Wife, Daughter, One Green Eye and I will bargain for a while. The two of you should go to the old women's fire to talk of things that make women laugh…and brave men uneasy."

One Green Eye sat himself across the fire from Standing Bear and behind him, the others sat cross-legged on the ground as well.

Long Feather and Smiling Moon each grabbed a buffalo hide from inside the lodge and headed toward where the old, widowed women lived together and kept their fire. Knowing One Green Eye was bargaining for a wife, the men would come here to watch the war of words and wills at Standing Bear's fire. Whereas the village women would head to the old women's fire until the bargaining was done. The women knew that once a bargain was struck loud cheers and whoops would be heard from the men at the bargaining fire.

So, until that time came, they would enjoy a chilly, clear evening with their friends. Once settled in, women eagerly began giving marital advice to Long Feather. As the night passed, their advice and stories covered subjects from cooking to digging salt, jerking meat, storing food, and maintaining a lodge. Most of which she had already learned from her mother over the years and from the women she had been working with in the village recently.

As the fire burned down, talk shifted to issues of a more personal nature. Being with child, childbirth, and caring for children became the subjects of serious discussion and sometimes laughter. Some advice interested Long Feather, and some terrified her. After that discussion played out, the women's talk turned to men and husbands, becoming much bawdier. The longer it progressed, the more some women began looking toward the distant group of men with irritation and longing in their eyes. No doubt there would be sounds of love play in some lodges tonight.

The full moon was high in the starry sky when the men's shouts and yells could be heard reverberating through the village. It was time to leave. The night was cold, and the women hurried to the warmth of their lodges and their sleeping pallets. Smiling Moon and her daughter also headed toward their lodge curious to hear the details of the bargaining.

When they arrived, Standing Bear was still sitting by the fire as they had left him. As the women approached, he looked up and gave them a sly smile as if to say, "One Green Eye is not as wise as he thinks." He spoke to his daughter. "Sit by the fire a moment, daughter. I will speak with you."

Long Feather, still wrapped in the buffalo hide, stopped and returned to the fire as her mother continued into the lodge. She sat where he had patted the ground beside him.

He stared into the fire's embers, speaking. "One Green Eye complained you were too headstrong to be a good wife. He also said that he would have to beat you often to make you mind his word." He gauged his daughter's reaction, who showed no outward response to his words, but she chuckled in her mind. She stared at the fire imagining One Green Eye's frustration during the bargaining with her father. "I told him that as a wife, you will bathe at the river with other wives. I also warned him that for every mark seen on your skin, I would put two lumps on his head with a rock."

She glanced over at her father with a wide smile on her face. Without hesitation, she spoke. "I promise that once I become a wife, I shall honor you Father and I will do my best to be a good wife and bear many grandchildren." In her mind, she pictured herself and Blue Stone and truly meant every word of her promise. Her eyes stung as she stood, touched his shoulder, and walked toward the lodge. At the door, she stopped and turned to take in the sight of her father sitting by the cooling fire.

He sat tall and proud. A slight smile was on his face as he closed his eyes and rocked gently, singing softly to himself. She strained as hard as she could to hold onto that memory of him. It would be the last time she would ever see or speak to him again.

Long Feather awoke with a start. The lodge's darkness told her that it was still night…her last night. Her cream of One Green Eye tying a strap around her neck and the other end to a tree with his dogs was so real that it had scared her awake. She lay there in the darkness, feeling her heart beat hard in her chest. She touched her neck, expecting to find the strap still there. But she felt nothing except her sweaty skin. Her breathing began to slow. Her fear and anticipation of leaving were greater than she had realized.

Soon, she could begin her new life with Blue Stone, sweeping the memory of One Green Eye from her thoughts and dreams forever.

Though too dark to see, she could hear her father's slow, rhythmic breathing as he slept. She couldn't hear her mother, but she knew she would be huddled close against her father with either a leg or arm draped over him.

The faint sound of twigs breaking told her that someone was walking past their lodge outside. Likely someone was going to the village's edge to make water like her father often did when the nights were cold. But the footsteps stopped near their lodge's hide door as if they had paused to listen to something. After a few moments, the walking continued until the sound faded into the distance.

Long Feather rose from her warm pallet and crept to the door. She pushed the hide aside to peek out into the village. On the eastern horizon, the barest beginnings of a faint pink glow whispered the sun was not far behind. No one moved near any firepit that she could see, so people would probably awaken later this morning after the late night of bargaining and women talk. Even the old men hadn't appeared as they usually did before dawn.

Ducking back inside, she stepped back to her pallet. She

picked up her joining blanket and reached toward where she had left her berry basket. Sure enough, she touched the handle with a fingertip and adjusted her hand to grasp the handle with a slight crunch. With the blanket and basket in hand, she crept through the hide door to stand full in the cold predawn morning.

Wrapping her blanket around her shoulders, she walked toward the trail that would take her to the riverbank. Stopping she realized the walker who had passed their lodge had not come back. So, fearing she might meet them walking back, she decided to go around their lodge and take a different path out of the village. That would surely keep the walker from ruining her careful plan.

Just outside the village, she stood motionless for a few moments, testing the air for sounds of movement. Hearing none, she headed through the small stand of woods to the river trail on the other side.

The sky glowed a brighter pink as she hurried down the river trail. She could imagine Blue Stone running through the woods to the river, then scanning the far shore for her blue and white blanket. She hoped he would still cross the river for her as the thought of going back to the village and One Green Eye made her heart sink. She had a moment of terror when she thought that it might still be too dark when he got to the riverbank. He might miss her blanket. But she calmed herself, knowing he would surely look until the sun had completely risen, and he couldn't miss her bright blue and white blanket then.

Suddenly, a strong arm reached around her waist from behind, lifting her off the ground. Another arm wrapped around her shoulder and covered her mouth while she was carried off the trail into the woods. Surely this wasn't Blue Stone.

She got her answer as she was thrown hard onto the ground. She hit on her side as the wind was knocked from her lungs.

Laying there dazed and gasping for breath, she saw a dark shape looming over her. The dark shape placed a large, hide-wrapped stick, sideways into her mouth and tied straps quickly behind her neck. Breathing through her nose now, she tried to reach up and pull the stick out of her mouth only to be rolled onto her chest while both of her hands were grabbed and pulled roughly behind her back.

A hide loop tightened around her overlapping wrists. Seconds later, another loop slipped over her feet and forced her ankles painfully together. She struggled and screamed, but only a few muffled sounds came from her gagged mouth. The harder she struggled, the tighter her hide bonds became.

Hands grabbed her shoulder and jerked her over onto her back. She looked up into the smiling face of One Green Eye, who was now partially illuminated by a pinkish-yellow sky glow shining through the trees above him.

She struggled against the straps while trying to curse him, but only dull sounds came from her mouth. With every second, she got angrier and thrashed harder, but he only watched and smiled his sadistic smile.

"Long Feather?" His eyes opened wide in mock surprise. "I was told by Standing Bear last night that you were going to the far end of the lake to gather berry skins to finish your joining blanket." He tilted his head and furrowed his forehead pretending poorly to look confused. "I came here to make water this morning, and I heard noises on the trail. Thinking I had been followed by a forest spirit, I hid and waited to capture it, but…it turns out to be my soon-to-be wife…" He knelt down on one knee beside the tied and gagged Long Feather, who looked up at him with blazing hatred in her eyes as she struggled to get free. He bent forward until his face was only inches from hers. His eyes were now cold and void of emotion. "Perhaps we should just wait here until the sun is bright and the morning is full. No one is looking for you to return home until the end of the day. We could just spend the time talking about our future children and even decide on a joining day." He looked at the gag in her mouth and smiled. "Though you wouldn't have much to say about either I'm afraid." He chuckled.

Long Feather's face showed fear as she imagined Blue Stone standing on the far shore, searching for her blue and white blanket. She could tell by the brightening dawn that she didn't have much more time to get there. People would be rising in the village and moving about. Twisting her hands and wrist behind her, she could feel how wet they had gotten from the morning dew. She moved her wrists around, trying to get the hide straps as wet as possible. She remembered the hide strap would slicken and stretch when it got wet. But would it happen fast enough for her to get free before Blue Stone gave up on her? But then she still had to overpower One Green Eye somehow and make it to the river in time. If she couldn't get to the shore soon, Blue Stone would leave, thinking she had decided to stay home and be One Green Eye's wife. The horror of that thought made her redouble her efforts to free herself.

"That would be a good day, wouldn't it?" he continued. His voice rising to an angry tone as he suddenly rose to a standing position beside her. He looked down at her with cruel eyes and an evil smile.

He picked up her joining blanket where she had dropped it on the ground. It hung limply from his hand, brushing the tall dewy weeds. The white part stood out against the green undergrowth and the forest shadows.

"But I must leave you to enjoy the morning by yourself." One Green Eye's tone turned casual. "Soon, I will bring Standing Bear here so that he can see for himself how you have spoken lies, plotted to shame him and broken his law." He turned away and walked toward the shore trail, leaving her to struggle on the damp undergrowth. But after two steps, he stopped and stood with his back to her and spoke. "Don't worry Long Feather," he spoke over his shoulder in a calm manner. "I will return with your father soon enough. But first I'll go to the big rock on the shore where I will wait for Blue Stone to come for you. And when he comes, I will kill him." He walked away without looking back. After reaching the path, he turned to follow it toward the riverbank and the big rock.

Blue Stone emerged from the forest trail. His friend, Red Fox, had attempted to follow him to the river. But upon being told by Blue Stone that he was going to wash himself and check the fish traps, he had visualized the icy water and decided to stay by the warm fire and wait for his friend to return.

Now standing on the riverbank, Blue Stone stared at the far shore, looking for the big rock near where Long Feather usually stood. After a few seconds, his eyes adjusted from the dark forest to the early dawn light, and he saw a bright blue and white shape on the other shore.

Instead of standing and waving as he had expected her to do, Long Feather sat on the shore with her blanket wrapped around her. It covered her entire body with just a small opening where her face would be. He decided she had probably been waiting for a while and had gotten cold in the morning air.

Thankfully, she had decided to go with him.

He waved an eager greeting and hand-talked, "Happy you here. Be there soon."

An arm extended partway out the small opening and waved slowly in response before retracting back under the blanket. Her response seemed odd, given their past interactions, but the sun was getting higher, and he needed to get across the river.

He hoped she was as eager as he was to begin their trek south before anyone looked for them. He trotted along the riverbank, heading to a location farther upriver. After a short time, he arrived at the place he had prepared the day before. On the shore lay a large, bare tree limb with half of it laying on the shore and the other half floating in the frigid water. He had found the dead, fallen limb in the forest and had dragged it here. By its size, he felt certain it would be enough to keep him from falling prey to the river demons that sometimes pulled his people under the water, never to be seen again. He had chosen this upriver location since he had previously dropped large sticks into the moving water and watched where they drifted. It was from this point that he had seen the dropped sticks float to the opposite shore quickly.

Taking a deep breath, he prepared not only for the cold river but possibly for a fight with a river demon. Walking waist-deep into the river, he pulled the dead branch free of the shore and pushed it out into the current. Once the current caught the branch, he threw himself atop the now free-floating branch. As expected, the freezing water washed over him, which made him inhale sharply. But as he had hoped, the branch kept his head and shoulders above the water.

He drifted toward the middle and fastest part of the river, and he knew this was where a river demon was most likely to strike. With that thought in mind, he tightened his grip on the limb and tried to keep his legs near the surface and out of reach. He closed his eyes and felt his heart pound, expecting boney claws to encircle his ankles at any moment...

But a handful of heartbeats passed, and nothing happened. He opened his eyes and noticed he was past the middle of the river. He drifted near the opposite shore. Just a few moments more and he would be safe in the shallow water, out of reach of the river demons.

Twisting her wrists in opposite directions, Long Feather felt the wet, slick hide straps stretch a little more. She was surprised at how fast they had absorbed the dew off the grass and weeds beneath her. But it felt like it was taking forever for them to stretch. It wouldn't be long before the combination of stretching and twisting her wrists would allow her to pull one hand free. With her hands free, she could remove the gag, untie her ankles, and run to face One Green Eye on the riverbank. Getting free was taking too long.

Her mind searched for a way to stop him once she got free. She knew she was not physically strong enough to take him on face-to-face. As her hand was nearly free, she had an idea. She would find a large, thick stick about as long as her arm. Armed with the club, she would run down the trail to a place short of the big rock. There, she would turn back into the forest and sneak her way through the trees to a spot behind where One Green Eye was hiding. Once she located him, she would quietly work her way out of the trees and onto the open shore where she would hit him with the club. After he was subdued, she would wait for Blue Stone, and they would decide what to do with him before they headed south.

As she finished formulating her plan, a hand slipped free. Sitting up, she brought her hands around to her lap and tried to unwrap the slippery straps from her other wrist. But with both hands numb from being bound tightly, any coordinated effort was difficult. Pretty soon, the tickle-needle sensation left, and normal feeling returned to her hands. She then freed her ankles and mouth. Getting to her feet shakily, she angrily threw the gag and wet straps as far as she could into the brush, steadied herself, and looked around for the club she had envisioned using to hit One Green Eye.

She spotted a pine limb on the ground half covered with brown needles. She walked over and picked it up. It wasn't as hefty as she would have liked, but it would work. She turned slowly, listening to the sounds around her. Confident she was facing the river's direction, she took off at a run, club in hand.

Blue Stone could see the gravel bottom moving beneath him as he drifted near the shore. Easing himself off the limb, he found his footing and stood thigh-deep in the water, a few feet from shore. Taking a quick glance down the river, he could see the big rock a short sprint down the now visible shore trail. He took three steps and was out of the river trotting down the trail.

The dawn sky was brighter now, and the pink glow had yielded to a brighter yellow of pre-sunlight. He had to hurry so they could make the most out of the day ahead of them. Not far ahead, he could see Long Feather still sitting on the trail, wrapped in her blue and white blanket. He felt his heart pounding with excitement at the thought of finally standing face-to-face with her, holding her hand. The months of watching, waving, and hand-talking across the river were finally at an end. Stopping in front of her, he dropped to his knees. As he leaned forward, he spoke to her softly. "Long Feather... It is I, Blue Stone. I'm finally here to..."

In a blur of blue and white, the blanket flew open, and he stared straight into the eyes of a strange man. He tried to understand what was happening. Who was this stranger, and what was so odd about his face? One answer quickly registered. One of his eyes was brown, and the other eye was green. Where was Long Feather.

A split second later, he felt a hard, painful pressure against his lower chest, and he knew something was wrong. He looked down and saw the uneven, bottom edge of a black buffalo horn...protruding from his upper stomach. He wanted to touch the horn to see if it was real, but his arms were now numb and hung useless at his sides. He felt a cold, overpowering weariness begin wrapping itself around him. As the bright sunrise darkened in his blurry vision, he was acutely aware that he could no longer feel his heart pounding with excitement. Blue Stone, proud son of Chief Red Bear, never felt the hard, damp earth on which he fell dead.

One Green Eye leaped to his feet and looked down at Blue Stone's limp body lying on his side beside the gurgling river. He chuckled, thinking Blue Stone had thought he could take what was rightfully his, but he had shown him that would never happen. Long Feather was his to do with as he chose, and the same fate would befall anyone else that tried to interfere.

Giving Blue Stone's body a curious nudge with his foot, One Green Eye turned away from the river and walked back toward the village. There, he would find Standing Bear and tell him of his daughter's deceit. He smiled, eager to see his shame when he brought him back to where he had left Long Feather bound in the woods. After collecting her, he would show him the body of the enemy he had killed and tell him their plan to defy his law and run away together. He mused cheerily that he would likely get Long Feather as a wife without having to trade anything for Standing Bear's blessing. No one else would want such a shameful and untrustworthy woman.

"This was a good day," One Green Eye thought. "A very good day indeed."

Slowing to a stop on the river trail, Long Feather could see the big rock in the distance. Likely her blanket was spread out on it as a signal. She had expected to see One Green Eye crouched behind it, waiting for Blue Stone's arrival, but he was not there. Where could he be? She took a few tenuous steps closer, while staying close to the wooded side of the trail. She was prepared to duck into the woods to avoid him if need be. She could now see down the trail and past the rock, but he could still not be seen.

She froze in terror, realizing he was likely hidden a few steps into the woods after spreading out her blanket for Blue Stone to see. With that in mind, she made her way slowly forward while carefully searching the woods' shadows for One Green Eye's form.

Closer to the rock now, she still couldn't spot him hiding in the shadows among the trees. She gave the big rock, now to her right, a quick sideways glance. Something blue on the far side of the stone caught her eye. Another step forward and another sideways glance. She saw her blanket lay crumpled in the dirt with an arm across it.

Completely forgetting about One Green Eye, she dropped

her makeshift club and ran to the far side of the rock. She fell to her knees hard beside the still form lying there. She reached out her shaking hands and rolled the body onto its back.

Blue Stone's lifeless brown eyes stared up at her. His hair and chest were still wet from crossing the river and his body was still warm to the touch. Sticking out of his upper stomach was what looked like the rough-edged bottom of a large animal horn. Grabbing it, she jerked it out of his body and dropped it onto her blanket. She carefully lifted his head and rested it on her thighs. Brushing the long, dark hair away from his face, she leaned in close as if expecting him to smile up at her, but no smile came to his lips, and no breath touched her cheek. She looked into his eyes again. They seemed frozen in surprise.

Gently, she closed them.

The numbness of shock slipped away, replaced by the cold chill and gut-wrenching feeling of loss. Her whole body shook uncontrollably, her eyes burned, and her breathing was ragged and uneven. A loud wail exploded from her throat, and she fell across his face, sobbing uncontrollably. As she cried, she picked up her blue and white joining blanket and wrapped it around her and part of Blue Stone as she knelt there on the riverbank.

The black buffalo horn she had dropped on her blanket clattered to the ground with the blanket's movement. Between sobs, she picked it up, recognizing that it was the buffalo horn One Green Eye had tried to give her two nights before. She then realized he had followed her to the river and had seen her hand-signing with Blue Stone. Knowing One Green Eye, he had probably followed her every time she came here and had seen when they had made their plan to run away. That was how he knew to follow her today. It was him she had heard passing her lodge just before dawn.

She stared at the blood-streaked horn in her hand and visualized how One Green Eye had enjoyed stabbing Blue Stone with the very gift he had offered her. She closed her eyes at the thought of how stunned Blue Stone must have been. Instead of finding her, a stranger had appeared and killed him with the black horn.

Her sobbing subsided, and her aching changed. Her old hatred of One Green Eye returned and smoldered again in her mind. The hatred was so strong that it filled her body and soul. She could see herself plunging the same black horn deep into his heart, while his evil smile morphed into an anguished scream as surprise filled his dying green eye. She could almost feel the pleasure of watching him crumple to the ground, dying in front of her village. Avenging Blue Stone felt right.

But then she thought of her mother and father standing among her people watching her kill One Green Eye, and the vision of revenge faded.

Long Feather knew in her heart that regardless of her hatred of One Green Eye and her grief for Blue Stone, she could never kill. She was nothing like One Green Eye. She also knew that such a death was too quick a punishment for all he had done. She could only hope that the Great Sky Spirit would one day make him atone for all the pain and sorrow he had brought upon others.

He was likely in the village now, telling her father about her lies and bragging that he had killed the outsider who had conspired with her against his law. In the end, he would not only be the village hero, but her father and mother would be forever shamed by her actions. And the worst part of it, she would *still* end up with One Green Eye.

She knew that now he could treat her as badly as he wanted

for the rest of her life, and no one, not even her father, would intervene. All she had done was bring shame on herself and her family.

All emotion drained from her body like blood from a wound. There was absolutely nothing left to do except sit with Blue Stone and wait for One Green Eye and her people to arrive. The lies and deception would be obvious to all. And so would begin the horror of the rest of her miserable life with One Green Eye.

She looked down at Blue Stone's peaceful face, thinking of their fathers' angry vows of long ago that had divided their people. Angry, selfish pride had driven everything to this moment. And in that moment, it came to her how she could save her parents from a life of shame and—more importantly—how to cheat One Green Eye out of ever possessing her.

One Green Eye cheerfully led the group along the river path toward where he had left Long Feather tied up in the woods. His story of her lies and her plan to run away with an outsider had thrown a dark silence over the group. Seeing the look of hurt and shame in Standing Bear's eyes had made this day well worth it for him.

Chief Standing Bear and Smiling Moon walked behind him, and many villagers behind them, eager to see the proof of One Green Eye's dark story.

At a point where Long Feather's berry basket lay on the trail, One Green Eye turned away from the river and walked a short distance into the woods, followed by the group. He stopped and looked around at the ground and flattened undergrowth. But Long Feather was nowhere to be seen. "This is where I left her bound when I went to meet Blue Stone," he stammered as he knelt to feel the pressed vegetation.

Now Standing Bear looked at the disturbed and flattened undergrowth and scanned the area around it. "This looks like a deer bedding to me," he said flatly, and most of the other men nodded in agreement. "I see nothing that proves Long Feather was ever here." He gave One Green Eye a stern questioning look.

Standing there with a truly confused look on his face, One Green Eye turned and walked back to the river trail with the group still in tow. On the worn path again, he turned and trotted toward the big rock where he knew Blue Stone's body would be waiting. His body lay on his back with an almost bloodless wound in his torso. And beside him, lying face down, her body partially covered with the crumpled blue and white joining blanket, was Long Feather. Her body was perfectly still.

Standing Bear strode forward, shoving One Green Eye to the side as he knelt beside his unmoving daughter. He took her shoulders and turned her over into his arms. Her skin felt warm against his bare arms in the morning chill. Her eyes were closed, and her arms lay limply by her sides. An ugly, black horn stuck out of her upper stomach. Its rough bottom edges were caked with damp earth. He gently pulled the horn from her body and looked at it with immediate recognition.

Smiling Moon rushed forward and fell to her knees beside Standing Bear, who still cradled his daughter's body with one arm while holding the black horn in the other. She carefully took her daughter from her husband, hugging her close to her chest as she rocked and wailed.

As if on some unheard signal, Standing Bear and all the other people shifted their gaze to One Green Eye, who now leaned on the big rock with confusion still on his face and now there was real fear in his eyes.

Standing Bear rose to his feet, dropped the horn, and faced One Green Eye.

One Green Eye shook his head in obvious disbelief, wringing his hands together. "She can't be dead," he mumbled. "She loves me, not him. He was bad. He was from across the river! Y—you said so yourself. She couldn't ever want him… I had to make sure they could not be together. The horn was… It was a gift I gave her. She's mine. She'll always be mine. No one else can have her! No one…no one…" he trailed off, shifting his bulging, crazed eyes to Smiling Moon rocking Long Feather's body. His whole body shook uncontrollably and he mouthed silent words to himself.

Standing Bear no longer heard One Green Eye's senseless babbling. All he knew was that his daughter was dead, killed with the buffalo horn that One Green Eye had offered to her as a present. He raised his hands as he took a measured step toward One Green Eye.

In that moment, a blinding flash of white light and instant, multiple, deafening cracks of thunder made everyone drop to the ground, covering their heads with their arms. With another great clap of thunder and accompanying flash of light came a roar of wind and torrent of rain so heavy that no one dared to raise their head. As the tempest swirled and beat down on them, the ground began to vibrate and shake. A third and final clap of thunder and flash of light assaulted their senses, and the rain and wind disappeared, leaving the sky instantly cloudless and blue.

Standing Bear was the first of the rain-soaked and terror-stricken people to raise his head and look around.

Where Blue Stone's and Long Feather's bodies had laid on the blue and white joining blanket all were gone. In their place was now a carpet of bright blue and white flowers. Anywhere there had been bare earth was now taken over by these strange flowers that Standing Bear had never seen before. Flowers now occupied the place where One Green Eye had stood cowering against the big rock. He was nowhere to be seen. As Standing Bear looked across the river, he saw the strange flowers had appeared there as well, spreading all along the far riverbank.

Standing Bear, Smiling Moon, and all the villagers got to their feet and looked at the river, seeing that it had been transformed as well. Large, flat boulders were now where there had been only deep, rushing water. The huge stones were evenly spaced and formed a path of giant stepping-stones that connected one shore to the other. The river rushed and swirled around the newly placed stones.

Smiling Moon asked, "Where did they go?" She was looking down referring to the now missing blanket and bodies.

"The Great Sky Spirit took them," Standing Bear said reverently watching the flowers spreading everywhere before his eyes. "The new flowers are the colors of Long Feather's joining blanket. He's telling me that because my vow forbid them from being together here, he took them to be together with him." He lowered his head in shame and sorrow.

"And what of One Green Eye?" asked one of the villagers standing behind him.

"I believe the Great Sky Spirit took him to punish him in some way unknown to us." He mused dully, through the pain of guilt, raising his gaze to again look at the river.

Coming out of the forest trail on the far bank was Chief Red Bear, followed by his people. They looked at the changed river and the spreading flowers with frightened looks. It was obvious from their frazzled appearance they too had experienced the angry intervention of the Great Sky Spirit.

Seeing Red Bear across the river, Standing Bear tentatively

raised his hand in a weak greeting and stepped carefully onto the first boulder off the shore. Feeling the solid rock, he began to make his way across the boulder path. Red Bear answered with his own wave, and he also stepped onto the stone path and began making his way to meet his long estranged friend. As they met on the largest stone in the middle of the river, they grasped each other by the shoulders and stared into each other's tear-filled eyes.

"The Great Sky Spirit spoke to us," said Red Bear referring to the lightening, thunder and rain. "Then he sent strange flowers to lead me to the river. I followed them, and the closer I got, a great sadness swept over me. And when I saw you standing on the other shore, I took heart as I saw you wave."

"The Great Sky Spirit spoke to me as well," said Standing Bear with tears streaming down his cheeks. "Because of our angry pride and stubbornness, he has taken from us that which was most precious." He lowered his eyes before continuing. "And he sent these flowers, so that we would know shame for the selfish pride that drove us to divide our people."

The two friends walked together back to where Long Feather and Blue Stone had died side-by-side on the blue and white joining blanket. The people of both villages watched and knew the two friend's vow of division would be no more forever.

The Great Sky Spirit sadly smiled to himself at hearing Standing Bear's new found wisdom and watched as the friends walked together again. Though the price was too high he knew the lesson was learned and hoped it would never be forgotten.

He then turned his attention to One Green Eye. As punishment for the great jealousy and hatred that had led to Long

Feather and Blue Stone's deaths, he cast him into the dark, marshy forests of the land; cursing him to live forever as a great, hairy beast with an aching heart and only the memories of his evil deeds. He would be destined to always be alone, living in the shadows and watching over the new flowers when they bloom every spring hereafter.

And so, to make sure his children would forever remember Long Feather and Blue Stone's love, the Great Sky Spirit created the bluebonnet and spread them across the land where the two lovers had lived and died together. And to remind his children of what hatred and jealousy can do, he hid a tiny, black buffalo horn inside every beautiful blossom. A *secret* that has been all but forgotten over time.

So, if some day you decide to sit under a live oak tree with your children and tell them Long Feather's and Blue Stone's love story, don't forget to also show them the secret of the bluebonnet. Oh, and don't forget to mention the great, hairy beast named One Green Eye, who's still wandering around Texas watching over the bluebonnets.

And if that's not enough to make someone think twice about picking bluebonnets, remember my late grandmother's spirit is out there as well. And let me tell you from personal experience. If she sees you *pick'n* bluebonnets, she'll make One Green Eye seem like a big teddy bear.

You have been warned!

*See the Secret of the Bluebonnet
in the following picture.*

PICTURE OF BLUEBONNET COURTESY OF
THE LADY BIRD JOHNSON WILD FLOWER CENTER, AUSTIN, TX

EPILOGUE

Enrique Esteban sat gazing out the door of The Pelican Tavern, not far from the small lodging house where he stayed. He had arrived that morning on the merchant ship, *Widow's Revenge*, after an uneventful voyage from Lisbon. After overseeing the unloading of cargo, he had made his mark, drawn his pay, and been told by the captain to be back early next Monday.

Grabbing his worn and patched sea bag, he had gone ashore and made his way to the small lodging house where he had stayed before. Fortunately, the one available room was unrented, and a shiny new shilling had secured the room for three nights and included one hot bath. So, he had almost three days to enjoy himself before he had to go back to the ship. He looked forward to enjoying a hot bath, a feather bed, some good wine, and kind attention of perhaps a señorita or two.

His many years as a sailor showed in the deep wrinkles etched into his brown, wind-toughened face and the scars on his body. He could see the docks and the river darkening from where he sat. Between the growing darkness and the arthritic ache in his hands and elbows, he knew rain clouds were set-tling in over London.

Though rainy weather brought the predictable physical discomforts of age, he always liked the world after a good rain shower had washed it clean. On a ship, the fresh rain washed away all the smells of a ship too long at sea, smells he was used to but didn't mind losing for a brief while. He and most of the crew would often stay on deck during a warm rain to have the sweat, grit, and salt washed from their hair, skin, and clothes. He knew a good rain would be a welcomed gift to the over-crowded city choked with the smells of garbage, horse dung, piddle, and coal dust.

He felt a cool breeze, that signaled the rain's arrival, blow through the door and across his tanned face. He closed his eyes and took in its freshness as he had done a thousand times before. He loved the wind; it was what he liked most about being a sailor. Even as a child, it had always fascinated him. How could something that could gently brush his face or fill a ship's sails be felt and measured but never be seen? That was the magic of the wind, and he loved it.

His thoughts were interrupted by large rain drops splatting on the worn flagstones outside the tavern door. Quickly, the rain's intensity grew until blinding sheets of it blew across the docks and the river. Occasionally, a misty puff of wind blew through the open door and onto his waiting face, and each time, he closed his eyes and enjoyed it.

"Allow me to close that door, sir, as I see you are getting damp from the rain blowing in," said his young host. He roughly set down the wine pitcher with a loud thump as he hurried for the open door.

"Please no, señor. Leave it open," Enrique said, stopping the young man's motion. "I like the sound of the rain and the feel of the wind. If you sit across the table from me, you should avoid any of the wind or dampness." He gestured with open hands at the chair across the small, rickety, stained wooden table. He tried his best to be polite to the fancy young man who he bet had more coin than calluses. He had spent the last few hours telling stories and had been generously rewarded with his cup being constantly filled with good French wine. Wine he could never have afforded with the thin purse he carried.

The young man had approached him when Enrique first entered the tavern. He had been eager to know his occupation. When Enrique had told him he was a sailor, the man had fallen upon him like a seagull on a dead fish, offering to keep him in wine if he would share stories of his life and travels. He was eager to hear tales of the people he had known, the women he had loved, and the places he had been.

And of course, being an accommodating man and a parched and underfunded sailor, Enrique felt sure they would both benefit from the proposed arrangement.

"Señor William," said Enrique, remembering the young man's name. "Why do you want to hear my stories? I am but an old sailor. You live here in London, one of the busiest cities in the whole world. It's filled with countless people to drink with and talk to. Why choose me and my old stories?" He queried, sincerely baffled by the situation. "Don't misunderstand. I will gladly drink your wine. It just seems a little crazy to me."

William shook his head and waved his hand in an overly exaggerated protest. "To be perfectly clear sir, I am not a Londoner. I live in this city only in part as I have rooms where I stay when working and seeing to my business here. My true home is a sleepy hamlet some three days' ride from here. I doubt you've ever heard its name as it boasts no great history or storied personages. The village is called Stratford, and it sits on the shore of a small forgotten tributary of the River Thames called Avon.

"And as to my interest in your wonderous stories, I am a man driven to search for new tales that none have heard before. You see, sir, I live to hear the tales of mad noble persons, restless and vengeful spirits, and human dramas heretofore unimagined by the masses. The stories of this town are many indeed… But they are ancient, and threadbare from the telling and retelling. Unfortunately, most are also known to all. You see, sir, I too am somewhat of a storyteller, and I am always seeking new fodder I can use or perhaps adapt to my humble storytelling." He smiled and waved his arms in a beckoning motion to Enrique. "So, fear not my expectations as I have none. I am truly your rapt audience for as long as my coin lasts or your tongue cares to wag. So, I humbly beg you, regale me, sir." That said in an overly dramatic tone, the young man sloppily filled Enrique's and his cups with hearty wine. He planted both elbows upon the table and rested his chin upon his interlaced fingers.

Completely satisfied with young William's explanation, Enrique stared up into the air for a few moments as if trying to recall an old memory. He smiled and nodded briefly then leaned across the table looking around the tavern in an almost conspiratorial manner. "The story I am about to tell you, señor, is one that I have never told a soul before. This tale is recorded in the travel chronicles of Franciscan monks and stored away in their dusty catacombs. The tale was recorded by the very monks that accompanied de Soto on his search for riches in the New World. The story was told by the people who lived in the Southwest, just north of New Spain. It's said to be a very, very old story, having been passed down for as long as the local people could remember. My older brother was a Franciscan monk. God rest his soul." The sailor crossed himself in memory of his late brother. "And he told me this story soon after the monks returning with de Soto from New Spain shared it with him."

He paused and leaned in a bit closer, again looking left and right. William matched his movements from across the table as if making doubly sure they weren't being spied upon.

"This story is a truly ancient one, señor. It's a tale of angry pride among leaders that divided a people. A story of…deceit, jealousy, hate, that caused the sad deaths of innocent and forbidden lovers. A story of a magical spirit that could throw lightning, change men into beasts, and turn the earth azure. This, my young friend, is a legendary love story that can never be forgotten once heard."

William's eyes twinkled with anticipation in the dim, smoky candlelight of the tavern. Outside, a blinding flash of lightning struck somewhere close, and the deafening crack of thunder echoed across the river Thames, as the old Spanish sailor told his story.

AUTHOR'S DISCLAIMER

The story presented herein is a fictional tale based on an oral story told to the author by a family member during his childhood. Any resemblance to people (living or dead), names, places, or historic information (written or oral) that appear in this story is unintentional and coincidental.

BLUEBONNET FLOWER FACTS

The bluebonnet was adopted as the Texas State Flower in 1901, beating out the Prickly Pear Cactus Flower. There are five varieties and several colors: purplish-blue, red, and white. The flower was also known by other names such as Wolfe Flower, Buffalo Clover, El Conejos (The Rabbits), and Azulejo Silvestro (Blue Wildflower).

It is not against the law to pick bluebonnets in Texas, except on private property or anywhere picking the flower is posted as prohibited. Also, stopping to pick bluebonnets can be dangerous since parking on the shoulder is unsafe, stinging insects often fly around the flowers, and poisonous snakes could be looking for rodents among the flowers.

The entire bluebonnet plant is toxic to humans and animals if eaten. Cattle, deer, and most insects avoid eating them, except in times of high environmental stress. Wash hands well after handling the flower.

Bluebonnet seeds germinate in the fall, bloom in late March, and fade in April, depending on variables such as moisture and sun exposure. They *can* be grown from planting seeds, but follow planting instructions carefully for the best results.

Bluebonnets and other wildflowers are planted along Texas highways for beautification purposes. The Texas Department of Transportation plants some 30,000 tons of wildflower seeds along its highways every year and avoids mowing the planted roadsides until after the spring wildflower season.

Bluebonnets are responsible for multimillions of dollars in Texas tourism every year.